The Little King Takes Back his Kingdom

By Nuha Sbeih

Illustrated by Noha Gmal

I am the **King**, with a kingdom to rule!
My home's in the center, with windows and a door so cool.
A giant oak tree stands tall and proud
With a well and stone steps rising from the ground,
And a horse, too, waiting to run around.
My grandpa's olive tree, a thousand years old
And jasmine flowers growing on the fence so bold.

Around the house, fields of mum flowers spread
Where I run and play, and the wind blows my head.
I laugh and laugh, and my whole kingdom laughs.
Everything is mine, for I am the **King**.

But then, some strangers came our way
And **stole** our kingdom, making us sway.
They hooked their weapons on the olive tree
And forced us to flee. . .

It happened so fast, I couldn't say goodbye
To my house, the oak tree, and my horse nearby.
I jumped out of bed and left my dreams behind
And I left the window **open**.

We walked and walked and walked through the night,
In forests, mountains, and the desert.
The grownups were feeling scared,
But we the little ones sang a song we shared:
"We'll be back home before too long,
To our kingdom where we all belong."

We sailed into the sea, and my crown was lost.
I didn't cry, but I knew the cost.
Perhaps my house, oak, jasmine, and horse
Were all crying, missing me, of course.

We arrived at the new kingdom, full of tents,
But it wasn't like the first, and we missed its scents.
My oak tree and grandpa's olives were gone.
I thought of my horse, I missed it all along.

Summer came and went so fast,
We sang, "We'll be back home at last."
Fall followed with its leaves of gold,
And we still sang, "We'll be back to hold."
Winter came, with snow and cold,
And still, we sang, "We'll be back to behold."
Now spring has come, without a bloom,
A whole year gone, as if shrouded in gloom.
Heavy time passed, and we longed for home.

As the **King**, I am **brave** and **strong**,
But sometimes even kings feel sadness prolonged.
"I miss my home, I am longing for it," I sang,
"My bed, my horse, and jasmine's sweet tang."

Then, a wind from my kingdom blew away
The scent of jasmine, bringing it my way.

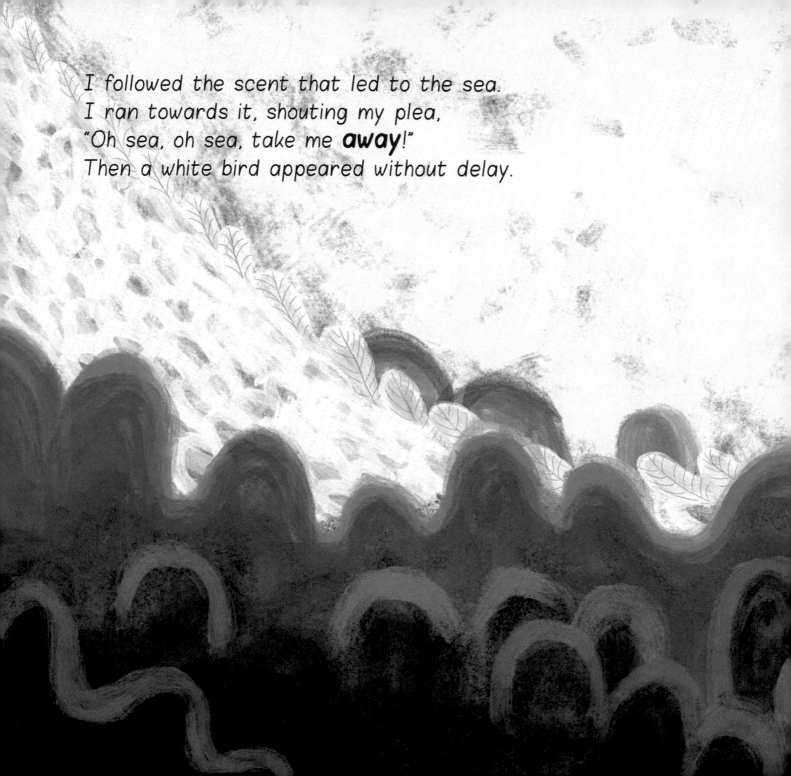

I followed the scent that led to the sea.
I ran towards it, shouting my plea,
"Oh sea, oh sea, take me **away**!"
Then a white bird appeared without delay.

A seabird, it perched, a companion for me.

I climbed on its back and off we flew,
Beyond the sea, to skies so blue,
Over the desert, mountains, and trees,
Together, we journeyed with the greatest of ease.

We arrived at the courtyard, where I saw my house,
The oak tree, the jasmine, and I hugged my horse.

The window was still open, the white bird had landed.
I slept soundly and happily, my sadness stranded,
As if I were riding the clouds, so high and free. . .
I am the **King**, and my kingdom is with me.

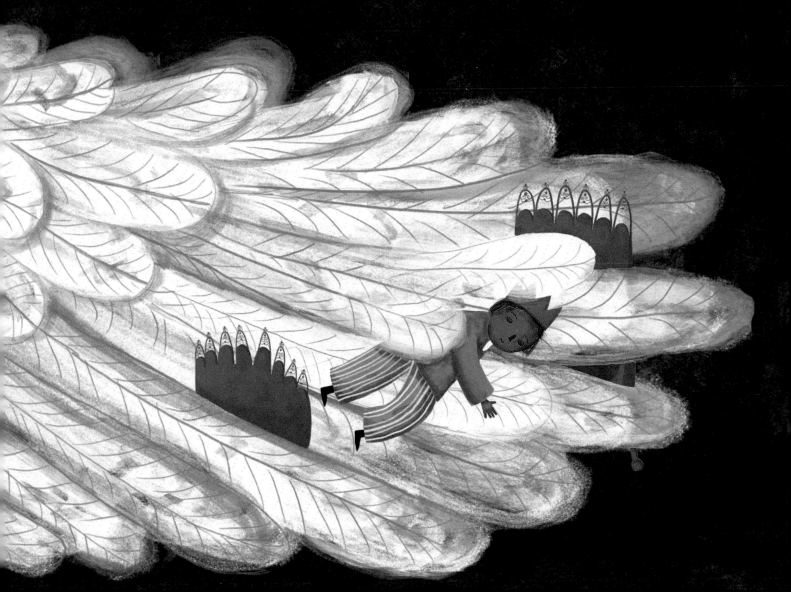

Translated by Ibrahim Akid
Art director Haneen Odetallah

Made in the USA
Las Vegas, NV
30 April 2023

71343958R10021